HENRY AND THE HIDDEN TREASURE

Copyright © B.C.R. Fegan 2017

Cover art and illustrations by Lenny Wen

The moral right of the author has been asserted.

HB — 978-0-9953592-4-6
PB — 978-0-9953592-5-3
Kindle — 978-0-9953592-6-0
EPUB — 978-0-9953592-7-7

Published by TaleBlade Press

TALEBLADE
www.taleblade.com

For Weeds — a sister as talented
and as caring as Lucy

HENKY AND THE HIDDEN TREASURE

B.C.R. FEGAN

ILLUSTRATED BY
LENNY WEN

TALEBLADE

Henry has a lot of treasure and
he keeps it very well hidden.

His parents call it 'pocket money' and wish that he would keep it in a bank.

Henry knows that only **he** can keep his treasure safe.

Henry has a problem.

His parents call the problem 'Lucy' and they think that he should be nicer to his little sister.

Henry knows his little sister is really a secret ninja spy sent to steal his treasure.

But Henry has a plan.

If it works, his treasure will be safe forever.

First, Henry will move all his
treasure into the secret cave.

Second, he will find the
darkest place in the cave
and hide his treasure there.

Third, his treasure will be guarded by a
giant and ferocious, pink pig.

Fourth, he will build a huge maze inside the cave. Anyone looking for the treasure will become completely lost.

Fifth, he will design some clever booby traps.

Sixth, he will make sure that the cave is guarded by an entire army of soldiers, monsters and superheroes.

Seventh, he will seal the cave
with a huge and very scary door.

Eighth, the door will be guarded
by a fire-breathing dragon.

Ninth, every path to the cave will be blocked by gigantic robots.

And tenth, if anyone
was quick enough,

and clever enough,

and strong enough,

and quiet enough,
and flexible enough,

and lucky enough,
and brave enough,

and prepared enough to find his hidden treasure...

Henry would be waiting with a powerful laser gun.

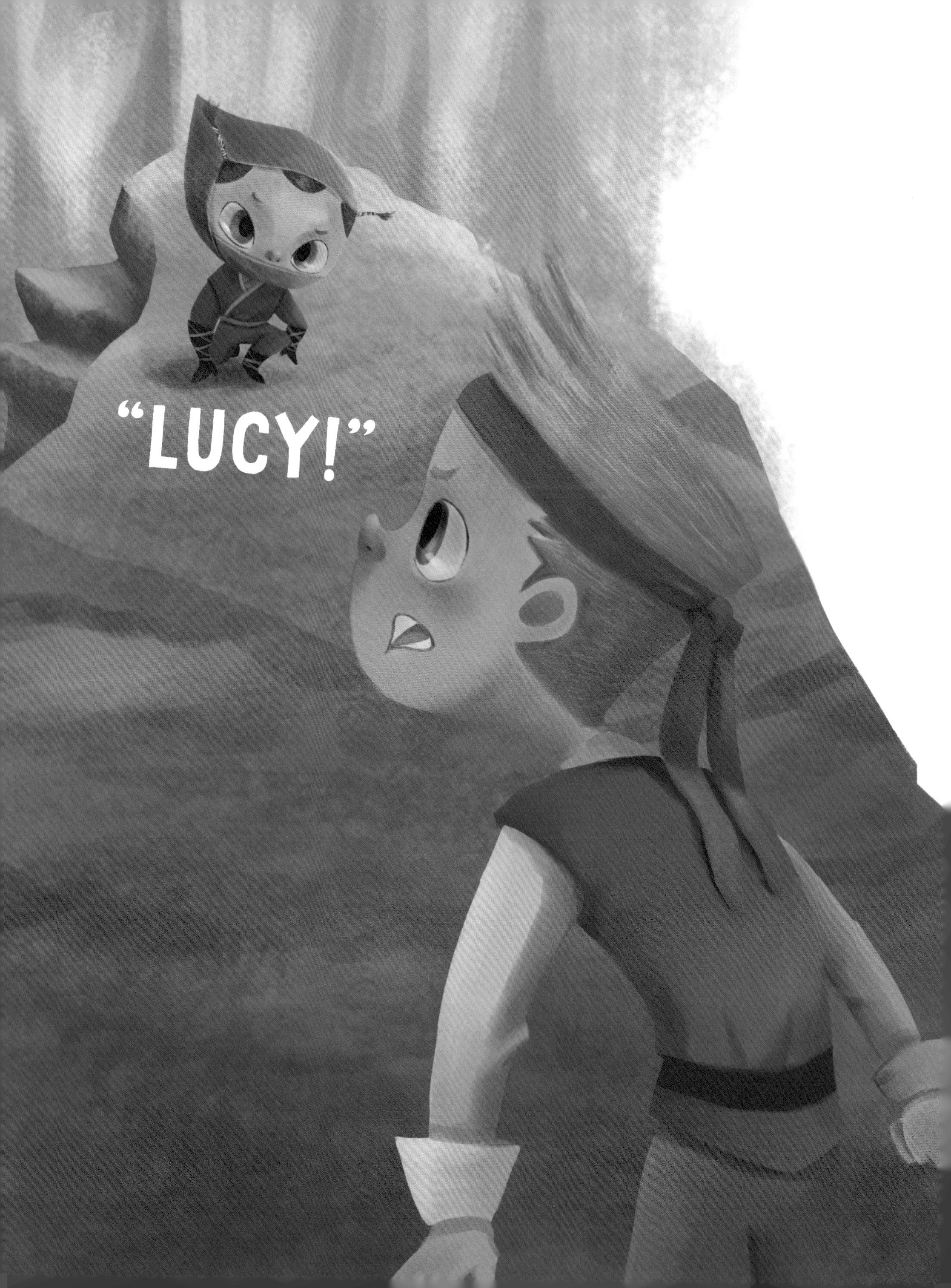

"LUCY!"

Lucy doesn't seem interested in Henry's treasure.

It looks like she fearlessly made it through everything just so she could give Henry ...

a hug!

Henry has a lot of treasure, but maybe
hiding it isn't the best idea.

Tomorrow he will put it in a bank.

But he might keep just enough ...

to buy Lucy an ice cream.

CPSIA information can be obtained at www.ICGtesting.com
Printed in the USA
LVIW01n2249171017
552824LV00006B/21